For Maria's cat, and Tawny Pippet, Ottoline, Nero, and Umblebee.   C.E.

For Colin, who was inspired to write this book on receiving one of my feline birthday greeting cards.
I also dedicate this book to all my family, especially Evan, James, and Julian, and to my mother,
and to all my cats, past, present, and future.   L.A.I.

Published by Dial Books
A Division of NAL Penguin Inc.
2 Park Avenue / New York, New York 10016
Published simultaneously in Canada by Fitzhenry & Whiteside Limited, Toronto
Text copyright © 1988 by Colin Eisler / Pictures copyright © 1988 by Lesley Anne Ivory
All rights reserved / Printed in the U.S.A. / Design by Ann Finnell
(b)
3 5 7 9 10 8 6 4 2
Library of Congress Cataloging in Publication Data
Eisler, Colin.   Cats know best / by Colin Eisler; pictures by Lesley Anne Ivory.
p.   cm.
ISBN 0-8037-0503-4   ISBN 0-8037-0560-3 (lib. bdg.)
I. Ivory, Lesley Anne, ill. II. Title.
SF445.7.E37 1988   636.8 — dc19   87-15653   CIP   AC

Some of the cats in this book live with the illustrator, Lesley Anne Ivory.
Their names, from left to right in the order of their appearance, are:

On the front cover: OCTOPUSSY (AGNEATHA's son)
On the title page: AGNEATHA
In front of the fireplace: TAM (MUPPET's son), and BRACKEN and D2 (AGNEATHA's sons)
Keeping cool: GEMMA (mother of MUPPET)
In the drawer: AGNEATHA and her kittens, and TWIGLET under the bed
Drinking milk: TWIGLET, and GABBY in the farmyard
Watching a mouse: TWIGLET again
Nursing her kittens: MUPPET and her kittens (GEMMA's daughter and grandchildren)
Keeping clean: GEMMA on the chair, and AVRIL and APRIL (AGNEATHA's daughters),
and MINOUCHE in the basket with PEEPO
Tidying up: SPIRO (the ginger cat) being groomed by BLOSSOM
Having a good fight: OCTOPUSSY and D2, with HOBOE, a neighbor, on the wall
Moving through the snow: MUPPET and her kittens; GEMMA, the grandmother, is on the windowsill
Playing cat's cradle: RUSKIN
Pretending not to care: CHESTERTON (TWIGLET and GABBY's son)
Looking back: CHESTERTON again
On the back cover: RUSKIN again

CATS KNOW BEST

by COLIN EISLER

pictures by LESLEY ANNE IVORY

DIAL BOOKS • *New York*

Cats know the best places to be.
Where to stay warm…

Or keep cool.

And where to have their kittens.

Cats know the best food.
Where the milk is freshest...

Or the mice most plump.

And how to nurse their kittens.

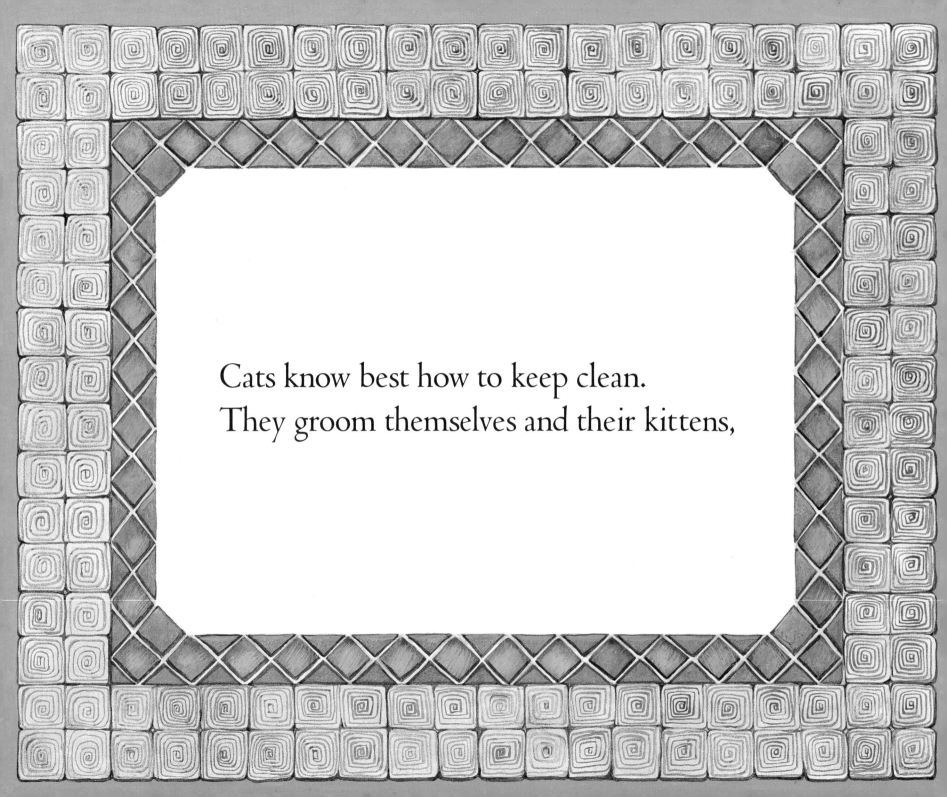

Cats know best how to keep clean.
They groom themselves and their kittens,

Helping each other keep tidy too.

Cats know the best feelings.
They love to have a good fight,
teasing and scrapping,

And caring for their kittens.

Cats know the best games.
They love to play cat's cradle,

And to pretend not to know, or to care,

But they do.